MAGIC
BONE

CATCH THAT ~~DOG~~ WAVE

For Bonnie Bader, editor extraordinaire, who never lets my writing
go to the dogs—unless it's supposed to!—NK

To Fin and Queenie—SB

GROSSET & DUNLAP
Published by the Penguin Group
Penguin Group (USA) Inc., 375 Hudson Street,
New York, New York 10014, USA
Penguin Group (Canada), 90 Eglinton Avenue East, Suite 700,
Toronto, Ontario M4P 2Y3, Canada
(a division of Pearson Penguin Canada Inc.)
Penguin Books Ltd, 80 Strand, London WC2R 0RL, England
Penguin Ireland, 25 St Stephen's Green, Dublin 2, Ireland
(a division of Penguin Books Ltd)
Penguin Group (Australia), 707 Collins Street,
Melbourne, Victoria 3008, Australia
(a division of Pearson Australia Group Pty Ltd)
Penguin Books India Pvt Ltd, 11 Community Centre,
Panchsheel Park, New Delhi—110 017, India
Penguin Group (NZ), 67 Apollo Drive, Rosedale, Auckland 0632, New Zealand
(a division of Pearson New Zealand Ltd)
Penguin Books (South Africa), Rosebank Office Park, 181 Jan Smuts Avenue,
Parktown North 2193, South Africa
Penguin China, B7 Jiaming Center, 27 East Third Ring Road North,
Chaoyang District, Beijing 100020, China

Penguin Books Ltd., Registered Offices:
80 Strand, London WC2R 0RL, England

Text copyright © 2013 by Nancy Krulik. Illustrations copyright © 2013
by Sebastien Braun. Published by Grosset & Dunlap, a division of
Penguin Young Readers Group, 345 Hudson Street, New York, New York 10014.
GROSSET & DUNLAP is a trademark of Penguin Group (USA) Inc.
Printed in the U.S.A.

Library of Congress Control Number: 2012032123

ISBN 978-0-448-46444-2   10 9 8 7 6 5

MAGIC
BONE

CATCH THAT DOG WAVE

by Nancy Krulik
illustrated by Sebastien Braun

Grosset & Dunlap
An Imprint of Penguin Group (USA) Inc.

CHAPTER 1

"Sit."

Uh-oh. What am I supposed to do when my two-leg, Josh, says, "Sit"? Is that the one where I dance on my back paws, or the one where I roll around on the floor, or . . . ?

I look around the room. What are the other puppies doing? It's hard to tell. They all look kind of confused, too. Boy, school is really hard.

Josh looks me in the eye. "Sit." He raises his hand.

I look up at his hand. Is there a

treat in there? I think there might be! I look up even higher and . . . *plop.* I land right on my rear end. Oh yeah. That's what *sit* means. "Good dog, Sparky," Josh says.

I smile. Those are three two-leg words I *definitely* understand.

But I don't sit for long. My paws start bouncing up and down. My tail goes crazy.

Oh boy! Oh boy! Oh boy! Josh is reaching into his bag. He's pulling something out. It's a . . .

Wiggle, waggle, whoopee! It's a liver treat! My favorite. I jump up and grab the treat from his hand. Treats are the best thing about school.

All around me, puppies are getting treats from their two-legs. I wish I could sniff the other puppies' butts and say hello. But I can't. At school, I'm only allowed to play with Josh.

Which is okay, because I *love* Josh. I also love that he's got that bag of my favorite treats. *Yummy, yum, yum.*

My tail wags harder. It's happy about the treat, too. Which is weird because my tail can't eat. It doesn't have a mouth.

"Sit," Josh says again.

Plop. I land on my rear end.

Josh reaches into the bag. Oh boy! Here comes another treat.

But Josh doesn't give me the treat. Instead, he holds it and walks away.

"Sparky, stay," Josh says.

I know what *stay* means. My paws have to be still and not follow Josh.

But Josh has that whole bag of liver treats. My paws can't be still. They walk toward him.

"Stay," Josh says again. But I don't listen. I *can't*. I want those treats!

My paws keep moving. Fast. Faster. *Fastest.*

My mouth starts barking. "Treat! Treat! Treat!"

Boom! I run right into Josh.

He falls down. And the bag of treats flies up! *Wiggle, waggle, woo-hoo!* It's raining liver!

"Piñata time!" Charlie the Chihuahua yips excitedly.

"Party!" Frisky the collie barks.

Soon all the puppies are barking.

"Treats! Treats! Treats!"

All the two-legs are shouting. "Stay! Stay! Stay!"

But none of us stay. How can we? There are treats *everywhere*!

My eyes see a treat in the middle of the room. My paws must see it, too, because they start to run right for it.

Frisky's paws run for the same treat.

Bam! Ow! We hit each other in the head.

Charlie sneaks in between us and grabs the treat.

"Hey, no fair!" I bark. "That was mine."

"No, it wasn't," Frisky barks back. "It was mine."

"It's mine now," Charlie says. He licks his lips. "And it's delicious."

Sniff, sniff, sniff. Wait. What's that in the corner? *Wiggle, waggle, wow!* There's a whole *pile* of liver treats there.

"Look out, liver; here I come!" I bark as my paws start to run to the corner. *Chomp!* My mouth scoops up the treats and my teeth start chewing. *Mmmm.*

"Bad dog, Sparky!"

Uh-oh. I understand those words.

But I don't like them. My tail doesn't like them, either. It sinks down between my legs.

I look up at Josh. "I'm sorry," I whimper. I cock my head and look extracute.

But Josh does not smile. He just says something to another two-leg.

That two-leg shakes her head and twirls her hand in a circle.

I know what that means! I get down on my belly and roll over.

But Josh doesn't smile. He doesn't call me a good dog for doing the roll-over trick. He just clicks my leash onto my collar and leads me out of the room.

Wiggle, waggle, uh-oh. I'm in trouble now . . .

CHAPTER 2

"So, it didn't go so well at school last night, huh, kid?" Frankie, the German shepherd who lives next door, says to me over the fence the next morning.

I look up from the hole I am *diggety, dig, digging* in the flower bed and shake my head. "Nope. But it wasn't my fault. Josh had *treats*."

"You're supposed to wait for your two-leg to *give* you a treat," Samson, the big mixed-breed who lives on the other side of the yard, says. "That's

what you learn in school."

"School," I bark back. "I hate that two-leg word. Whenever Josh says it, I run and hide. But he always finds me."

"You can't hide from school, kid," Frankie says.

"Frankie's right," Samson tells me. "Going to school and learning tricks is something every dog should do. It's good for us."

"Why?" I ask him.

"I don't really know, but it is," Samson says.

Wow. I thought Samson knew everything.

"Learning tricks isn't that bad," Samson continues. "It's the easiest way I know to get treats."

"I love treats," I admit. "But they don't love me. I ate *too many* yesterday. My stomach got all wiggly-wobbly. I left a pile of yuck on the floor of the car."

"Been there, done that," Frankie says. "How can something so good make you feel so bad?"

Samson yawns. "All this talk about tricks and treats is making me tired," he says. "I'm going inside to take a nap."

I know what Samson means. *Sit. Stay. Roll over. Heel.* Thinking about those two-leg words makes my head ache.

But I don't feel like napping. It's too early. Josh only *just* left in his big machine with the four round paws.

My paws think it's a good time to go back to *diggety, dig, digging.*

"You better stop digging up that flower bed," Frankie warns me. "You're in enough trouble with your two-leg already."

Oops. Frankie's right. Josh doesn't like when I dig up his flowers. And I've *duggety, dug, dug* up a whole lot of them.

"I'm going inside," Frankie tells me. "My two-leg had bacon this morning. I'm going to go see if she left any behind."

Frankie pads off into his house. Now I'm alone, with nothing to do. I've already *duggety, dug, dug.* I've already rolled in the mud. And I've already watered the grass—if you know what I mean.

Sniff, sniff, sniff. Just then, I smell something amazing. Like chicken, beef, and sausage all rolled into one.

I think the smell is coming from the big hole I've been digging. I look deep down. And that's when I see it. My *bone.* Buried under the flower bed. Right where I left it!

My bone isn't just any bone. It has magic powers. It can *kaboom* me right out of my yard! No, really. The last time I took a bite of my magic bone, it took me all the way to London!

London was fun—and *yummy, yum, yum.* You wouldn't believe the snacks they have in London. Sausages, cheese, and fish and *chips.* (That's what the dogs in London call fries.)

But London was scary, too. There were mean folks there, like the dogcatcher who threw me in the pound, and the Bulldog Boys. I *never* want to meet up with that gang of growlers again.

Sniff, sniff, sniff. My magic bone smells so meaty. I can't help myself. I just have to . . . *chomp!*

Wiggle, waggle, whew. I feel dizzy—like my insides are spinning all around—but my outsides are standing still. Stars are twinkling in front of my eyes—even though it's daytime! All around me, I smell food—fried chicken, salmon, roast beef. But there isn't any food in sight.

Kaboom!

CHAPTER 3

Wiggle, waggle, wow!

I'm standing in front of the biggest water bowl *ever*! It's so big that I can't see the edges. It just goes on and on and on. Good thing. Because I'm really thirsty!

Come on, paws! Let's go get some water!

Ow! Ow! Ooooo! My paws don't like this place one bit. This dirt is not soft like the grass and mud back home. It's hard and scratchy. And *hot*!

But the water is cool. And Josh isn't here to tell me "no!" when I step in the water bowl. In fact, none of the two-legs around here are telling me no. I think I'm gonna like this place—wherever it is.

I grip my magic bone between my front paws and drink.

Slurpity, slurp, yuck! My tongue gets all dry. The water burns going down my throat.

Burning water. Now that is really strange.

Spit, spit, spit. I can't get this water out of my mouth fast enough. *Spit. Splash. Whoa!* A big wall of water hits me, hard. It knocks me right on my tail. *Ouch!* I have itchy, scratchy dirt in places dirt should never go.

But I hold on tight to my magic bone. I don't want to lose it in the giant water bowl. If I did, how would I ever get home?

Shakity, shake, shake! I shake my body all around. Water flies everywhere!

A group of two-legs sitting nearby gets up and moves away from the giant water bowl. I guess they don't like the salty water, either.

Splash! Another big wall of water knocks me on my tail.

Wham! Water rushes into my ears and eyes, and up my nose. Wow, does it burn!

Aaachhoooo! I sneeze. The water rushes off me and back into the bowl. A big stream of goo drips out of my nose.

"Ha-ha, ha-ha!"

I turn around and see a Shiba Inu laughing at me. She sniffs my butt to say hello. "My name is Olina," she yips.

"I'm Sparky," I bark. I sniff her butt to say hello, too.

Olina laughs again.

"What's so funny?" I ask her.

"You are," Olina says. "You're covered with sand."

"Sand?" I repeat. "What's that?"

Olina paws at the scratchy dirt. "This stuff," she says. "And your fur is all soggy."

"That's not my fault," I insist. "Somebody must have tilted that giant water bowl. The water got all over me."

"Giant water bowl?" Olina looks confused. "Oh, you mean the *ocean*?"

"The *what*?" I ask her.

"The ocean," she repeats. "The *Pacific* Ocean. That water goes all around Maui."

Owie? I look at her strangely. An

owie sounds like she just got hurt. But she didn't even move. You can't get an *owie* if you're standing still. At least, I don't think you can.

"I get *owies* all the time," I tell her. "Yesterday, I was chasing a treat, and my fur got in my eyes, and I banged right, into a collie. *Owie!*"

Olina giggles again. "Not *owie*," she explains. "*Maui.* That's the name of this island. Don't you know anything?"

I know lots of things. I know I'm not supposed to jump on the couch. Or stick my snout in some other dog's pee when I'm out for a walk. And now I know that when a two-leg says, "Sit," you're supposed to plop down on your rear end. But I don't think that's what she means. I look at her, confused.

"Anyway, aloha, Sparky," she says to me. "Welcome."

"Aloha?" I ask her. "I thought you said Maui."

Olina laughs. Again. I don't like the way she's always laughing at me. It's not polite. Samson would have a thing or two to say to her about that.

"Maui is the name of this island," Olina explains. "Aloha is how we say hello here in Hawaii."

Hawaii? Aloha? Maui? I have trouble keeping all the words straight in school. But the words in this place are *really* confusing.

"Nice bone," Olina says, changing the subject. She points her snout toward my magic bone.

I step away with my bone. What if she takes it from me? How would I get back home?

But Olina doesn't go for my bone. She heads off after her two-leg instead. "Bye, Sparky," she barks as she runs.

I better bury my magic bone quick. Olina was little. And she didn't try to take it from me. But what if a big dog comes by who wants a taste? I'd be in real trouble.

Okay, *where* should I bury the bone? When I was in London, I buried it under a sign with a duck painted on it. That made it easy to find again. *Hmmm.* There aren't any duck signs here.

But there is a little wooden house with a whole pile of chairs outside. *Wiggle, waggle, perfect!* I'll bury my bone there! It will be easy to find when I'm ready to take a bite and go home.

Diggety, dig, dig. The sand flies all around.

I drop my bone in my great big hole. *Scratchety, scratch, scratch.* I turn around and use my back paws to scrape all that scratchy sand back into the hole. My bone is completely buried. No other dog will ever find it.

Rumble, rumble, grumble. That's my tummy talking to me. I speak tummy. So I know my tummy is telling me that it's hungry.

Good-bye, bone. I'll be back to get you later. Right now, I'm off on a new adventure! A yummy, *tummy* adventure!

CHAPTER 4

Sniff, sniff, sniff.

Wow! This place smells almost as good as my magic bone. I smell food everywhere! Chicken, fish, meatloaf. *Mmmm.* I think I'm going to like it on Maui!

The best part is that the two-legs are all sitting on blankets. I don't know why the blankets are on the ground. I thought blankets only went on beds. But here they go on the sand. And the two-legs are eating on top of them.

I know the rule. I'm not supposed to grab food from a table. But there are no tables. And anything that falls on the ground is mine if I want it. Everything here is on the ground. Which means I can eat *everything* these two-legs have. *Wiggle, waggle, woo-hoo!*

Sniff, sniff, sniff.

Mmmm. My nose knows when it smells something good. Right now it smells fried chicken. My tail starts wagging wildly. It likes chicken, too.

I spot the two-legs who are eating chicken. They are sitting under one of those things Josh holds over his head to catch the water when it falls from the sky. A lot of two-legs are sitting under water catchers. Which is strange, because there isn't any water falling from the sky.

But I don't care about the weather. All I want is that fried chicken.

Sniff, sniff, snag! My teeth grab a big piece of chicken. *Yummy, yum, yum!*

"No!" Just then, one of the two-legs jumps up on his two legs and shouts angrily.

But I don't stop chewing. He can't be talking to me. I followed the rule. The chicken was on the ground. It's mine.

Lots of two-legs are shouting. I don't understand what they're saying. But they sound angry. *Really* angry. My tail is scared. It tucks itself between my legs.

I look up, and they are all screaming—at me.

Come on, paws. We gotta get out of here. I drop the chicken and run.

Go, paws! Go!

Boy, do my paws go! Fast. Faster. *Fastest.*

I'm not sure where I am going. My fur is flying in my eyes. And I can't see a thing.

But my paws keep running away from the screaming two-legs. Fast. Faster . . . *Boom! Crash!*

Uh-oh! I just knocked over a giant water catcher.

Then that water catcher knocks over another one. Which knocks over another one. And another . . . *"No! Bad dog!"*

I know what those words mean. And I don't like them.

"It's not my fault!" I bark back at the two-legs. "I had fur in my eyes. And my paws wouldn't stop. Bad paws!" I bark at my paws. "Rotten fur in my eyes!" I bark at my fur.

One of the two-legs is coming toward me with his arms stretched out. He looks like he wants to grab me. Is he a dogcatcher like that two-leg in London?

I don't want to go to the pound! My tail hides farther and farther between my legs. It doesn't want to go to the pound, either.

A big two-leg jumps right for me. I leap out of the way.

Oomph. The two-leg lands

facedown in the itchy, scratchy sand.

Phew! He just missed me.

But now another two-leg is coming at me from the other side.

I leap backward. Scratchy sand flies into my mouth. *Ptooie!* I spit it out. Sand tastes even worse than burning ocean water.

The second two-leg turns slightly and . . . *Slam*! He trips over the first two-leg and lands right where his tail would be—if two-legs had tails.

I have to get out of here. My paws race over the hot ground. Scratchy sand leaps up into my eyes. It hurts, but I can't stop to rub it out. I have to keep going.

I run down toward the big water bowl that Olina called the ocean.

Then I *zoom, zoom, zoom* away from the screaming, falling two-legs and the giant water catchers.

I don't know the Hawaiian word for *dog pound*. And I definitely don't want to find out!

CHAPTER 5

Thumpety, thump, thump. My heart is pounding.

Scratchety, scratch, scratch. My fur is itchy.

My eyes are hurting from the sand that flew inside. And my mouth is really dry from drinking the burning water. I'm feeling pretty owie on Maui. I want to go home.

But to go home, I need my magic bone. And I can't go back to the sand where my bone is buried. Not with all those angry two-legs still there.

Luckily, I don't see any two-legs

around me. Now I'm in a place that has lots of giant green bushes and trees to hide behind. Instead of sand, there's soft mud under my feet.

Roll, roll, roll. I love rolling in soft, cool mud.

It's nice here. It's really quiet. Just me, the mud, the trees, and . . . *Owie!* I guess I'm not alone. There are bugs here, too. And one of them just bit me. *Itchity, itch, itch.* Get off my ear, stupid bug!

"Cheer wee. Cheer wee."

Gulp. What was that?

"Cheer wee. Cheer wee."

I look up in one of the trees.

That's when I spot him. A yellow-and-green bird. He's sitting on a branch, grabbing those owie-in-Maui bugs with his long hooked snout.

"Cheer wee. Cheer wee."

I want to tell the bird to be quiet. I want to tell him that I'm hiding. But I can't. I'd have to bark to tell him that. And then I wouldn't be quiet anymore. When you're hiding, you have to be really, really quiet.

"Cheer wee. Cheer wee."

Crunch, crunch. Crunch, crunch.

Uh-oh. I hear paws crunching the leaves that have fallen on the ground. And they don't sound like dog paws. They're two-leg paws. And they're coming toward me. *Gulp.* I hope those aren't dogcatcher paws I'm hearing.

"Cheer wee. Cheer wee." *Whoosh!* The bird flies away as the two-leg gets closer. I wonder if he's afraid that the two-leg is a *bird*catcher, coming to

get him. Is there such a thing as a birdcatcher? Or a bird pound?

Thumpety, thump, thump. That's my heart pounding.

Scratchety, scratch, scratch. That's me, scratching away another bug.

Crunch, crunch. Crunch, crunch. That's the two-leg coming closer.

"AAAAAHHHH!" And that's me barking as I come face-to-face with a two-leg. She's staring at me through the bushes.

But the two-leg doesn't scream back at me. She doesn't try to grab me. She just smiles and talks to me.

This two-leg is no dogcatcher. I can tell. She's young. Dogcatchers are grown-up two-legs. And her voice is too kind. I don't understand what this two-leg is saying to me. But I can tell she's being nice. Dogcatchers are never nice.

My heart stops *thumpety, thump, thumping* a little. But I'm still kind of scared.

The two-leg holds something out to me. *Sniff, sniff, sniff.* It smells sweet. I take a bite.

The treat is sweet, cold, and tangy. It's some kind of fruit. *Wiggle, waggle, yum!*

The two-leg pets my head and scratches behind my ears. I cock my head. "A little to the right, please," I bark. The two-leg scratches me again. She's a good head scratcher. Not as good as Josh, but almost.

The two-leg holds out another piece of the sweet, cold, soft treat. I grab it out of her hand, being careful my teeth don't hurt her.

Chomp. Yum. This juicy treat tastes so good.

"More! More! More!" I bark. My tail wags happily. It loves sweet treats, too.

The two-leg smiles and hands me another treat. Maybe she speaks dog. She sure understands what I am saying!

I take the treat from her hand and start to chew. But before I can even swallow, she starts to walk away.

What? "No!" I bark. "You can't leave. I have to have more!"

I guess the two-leg doesn't speak

dog after all because she keeps walking.

Suddenly, my paws are following the two-leg down the road. I don't even *try* to stop them.

Come on, paws! Follow that treat!

CHAPTER 6

I follow the two-leg up a hilly, muddy road. Well, actually I'm following the sweet, cold treats she keeps giving me, but it's sort of the same thing.

There are lots of trees along the road. Only they don't look anything like the tree in my yard. These have long, thick leaves just at the top. And there are big brown balls hanging from some of them. I wonder if dogs are allowed to play with them. I love playing fetch.

Suddenly, the two-leg stops walking. She hands me another cold, wet treat. I snap it up and start chewing. Sweet juice drips down my throat.

I look around as I chew. And that's when I realize that we're not alone anymore. The two-leg has stopped in a place where there are lots of other two-legs. *Gulp.*

I stand still and try not to cause any trouble. Trouble gets dogs put in the pound.

Just then, I see two other dogs—a Yorkie and a beagle. They run over to my new two-leg pal.

"Gimme some! Gimme some!" the Yorkie yips.

"Me too! Me too!" the beagle howls.

The two-leg I've been following holds out a piece of fruit. The Yorkie snaps it up quickly.

"Yum," she yips excitedly. "More! More!"

"I haven't had firsts yet," the beagle barks at her. "You can't have seconds before I have firsts."

"I can have anything I want," the Yorkie snaps back. "I'm cuter than you. And I just had a bath, so I'm cleaner, too. You smell like you just rolled in old poi."

I don't know what poi is. But I do know the beagle really does smell like he hasn't had a bath. I can tell because I'm busy sniffing his butt.

"Hello," I say.

"Aloha," the beagle answers.

"Who are you?" the Yorkie asks. "And where did you come from?"

How do I answer that? I don't want to tell the Yorkie about my magic bone. She might want it. She seems to want everything.

"I'm Sparky," I say, answering one question but not the other. I sniff her rear end.

"Aloha, Sparky," the Yorkie says. "I'm Darla."

"I'm Willie." The beagle sniffs my butt. "I've never smelled you before. You must be a new puppy."

Of course I'm new. *All* puppies are new. If we were old, we'd be dogs.

"You're lucky," Willie continues. "Lolani's nice."

"What's a Lolani?" I ask.

Darla looks at me like I have three heads. "Don't you know the name of your own two-leg?" she asks.

"Sure," I tell her. "Josh."

Darla looks at me like I have *four* heads and two *tails*. "What's a Josh?"

"My two-leg," I tell her.

Willie shakes his head. "I just saw you come in with Lolani. Aren't you her new puppy?"

I open my mouth to tell him no, but I shut it again just as quickly. If I tell Darla and Willie about Josh and my house with the yard that has a tree, grass, and flower beds, I will have to tell them about my magic bone. And I don't want any other dogs knowing about that.

So I don't say anything.

"You're lucky. Lolani is really nice," Darla says. "She's always giving us treats. Like that pineapple we just ate."

"But we're not getting Lolani's pineapple anymore," Willie tells Darla. "She'll give all her treats to Sparky now. He's her puppy."

Gulp. I don't like the sound of that. I'm *not* Lolani's puppy. I'm *Josh's* puppy.

I look over at Lolani. She's carrying something in her hands. It must be some kind of food, because she's licking it with her tongue—just like a dog.

"What's she eating?" I ask Darla and Willie.

Now Darla stares at me like I have four heads, two tails, and a *banana* for a nose.

"You've never had shave ice before?" she asks me.

"Nope."

"It's delicious," Willie tells me. "My two-leg, Hanini, shares hers with me all the time."

Darla pads over to her two-leg and starts licking her shave ice. Willie walks over to his two-leg.

"You don't know what you're missing, Sparky," Willie says between licks of Hanini's ice.

I guess the rules are different on Maui. Here dogs share food with two-legs. So I pad over to where Lolani is sitting, stick out my tongue, and *slurp*!

Wiggle, waggle, whoa! That's cold. *Really* cold. My tongue tingles.

My eyes bulge. And my head starts to ache.

"Sparky's having a brain freeze," Darla tells Willie.

"Happens to all the puppies the first time," Willie tells me. "You'll get used to it."

A second later my head warms up. Now all I taste is sweet *yummy, yum, yumminess.*

My tail leaps out from between my legs and starts wagging.

Lolani moves her shave ice away. I guess she's afraid my tail will want a taste, too.

"Stop it!" I bark at my tail.

But my tail doesn't stop. It keeps wagging.

I reach my head around and try

to grab my tail. My tail wags harder.

I reach. It wags. I reach. It wags. Soon my tail and I are running in circles.

"I'm gonna catch you!" I bark at my tail. My tail doesn't bark back. It can't. It doesn't have a barker.

It doesn't have paws, either. But that doesn't mean that it can't move away from me. It can. And every time I try to grab it, it wags a little faster.

Grab. Wag. Grab. Wag. Grab . . . *Splat!*

Wiggle, waggle, whoops! My tail smacks a shave ice out of the hands of a big two-leg on a bench.

Plop. The freezing-cold shave ice lands on the head of the little two-leg next to him. Cold, wet ice slides down his face and into his mouth.

"WAAAAAHHHH!"

The little two-leg starts to scream. His cries hurt my head worse than brain freeze.

The big two-leg glares at me and stands up. *Uh-oh.* This is the trouble I was trying not to get into. "Come on, Sparky," Darla calls to me. "We're leaving."

I'm not sure what to do. Darla and Willie are following their two-legs. But my two-leg isn't here. He's at home.

I guess I could go with Lolani.

The only trouble is, if I follow Lolani, Darla, and Willie, I might wind up so far from the sand that I never get my bone back. And then I might never get home to Josh.

The big, angry two-leg is heading my way.

"WAAAAAHHHH!" The little two-leg is still screaming.

Ow-ow-ow-ow! My head hurts. My ears hurt.

There's only one thing to do.

"Hey!" I bark to Darla and Willie. "Wait up! I'm coming with you!"

Darla and Willie stop for a moment, and I hurry to catch up.

"So where are we going?" I ask them.

"We're following the two-legs," Willie tells me.

"And where are they going?" I ask him.

"To hula," Darla tells me.

I don't know what hula is. Is it a thing? Another two-leg? A place? Are we following the two-legs away from Maui? Will I be leaving my bone behind?

All I know is that I can't stay here. So I follow Willie and Darla. My heart is *thumpety, thump, thumping.* I'm really scared about going to hula.

Whatever it is.

CHAPTER 7

"School?" I ask Darla and Willie a few minutes later. "I followed you to *school*?"

"Yup," Darla says. "*Hula* school."

I start to back away. "No way," I tell them. "Not me. I'm not going to school."

Willie scratches the back of his ear. "Me neither," he says. "It's not *dog* school."

"It's a different kind of school. Two-leg school," Darla explains.

Now it's my turn to look at her

like she has two heads. "There's no such thing as two-leg school," I tell her. "School is for dogs. That's where I learned to sit." I plop down on my rear end, just to show her. "And roll over," I add, rolling around and around in the soft grass.

Darla isn't impressed. "Well, *this* school is for two-legs. They're the ones doing the learning."

"What do we do while they're learning?" I ask Darla and Willie.

"I'm taking a nap," Willie says. He sprawls out on the ground.

A nap! That sounds *wiggle, waggle, wonderful*! All this walking around has made me tired. I lie down, shut my eyes, and . . .

"Cheer wee! Cheer wee!"

I look up into a nearby tree. There he is. My yellow-and-green bird buddy. He's singing and snacking on bugs.

"Cheer wee! Cheer wee!"

"Hi, bird buddy!" I bark.

"You know him?" Darla asks me.

"Uh-huh," I answer. "We were hiding together. Well, I was hiding. He was eating. And singing."

"I love that song," Darla says. "I don't hear it that often."

"Yeah, I don't see them around

much anymore," Willie agrees. He sounds sad.

"Why not?" I ask him.

"I don't know," Willie admits. "It's like one day they were here, and the next day they weren't."

"I miss them," Darla says. "They sing so pretty."

"Cheer wee! Cheer wee!"

I don't have much time to listen to the bird, because all of a sudden Lolani is standing in front of me. And she's carrying a big pile of grass.

At least it *looks* like a pile of grass. But it's not grass like I roll around in at home. This grass is dry. And it's tied to a string.

Lolani wraps the grass around my belly.

Wiggle, waggle, whoa! "What are you doing?" I bark.

Lolani doesn't answer. She can't. She doesn't know what I'm saying. She keeps wrapping the grass around me. Then she ties the string around my back.

Huh? What's going on here? Grass is for rolling in or digging up or peeing on. Not for this!

Lolani places a big circle of red and yellow flowers over my head and kisses my face. She smiles at me.

But Darla and Willie aren't smiling. They're laughing.

"You look ridiculous," Darla tells me.

Grrr. Darla is being mean. But she's right. I feel like I'm wearing a garden. This *is* ridiculous.

I bite at the grass with my teeth. But Lolani has tied it tight. *Bite, bite, bite.* It's not coming off.

I'm not the only one wearing grass and flowers. All the two-legs are wearing them, too. Two-leg school sure is different from dog school.

Or . . . maybe not. Lolani is moving her hands all around—just like Josh

does at *my* school.

Lolani raises her hand. Ooo! I know that one. That's *sit*!

Plop. I fall down on my rear.

I look up at Lolani and wait for my treat. But Lolani doesn't give me anything. Instead, she flips her hand over.

Hey. Wait a minute. This sure seems like my school. Are Darla and

Willie fooling me? Is this really dog school?

I look over at Willie and Darla. They're not learning. They're sleeping in the sun.

But Lolani is flipping her hand over again. And she's looking right at me. I'm not sure what kind of school this is. But I figure I better do what Lolani's hand is telling me to do.

Flop. I drop to the floor and roll over and over and over and . . . Whoops! I roll right into one of the other two-legs. "Sorry," I bark.

The two-leg growls something at me. She sounds a little like a dog. But I don't go over and sniff her butt. You don't sniff butts in school.

Lolani holds her fingers up in the

air. She spins them in a circle. I've never seen that sign before. But it has to mean something. Every sign means something when you're in school.

Thinkity, think, think. Up. Her fingers are up. Maybe I should go up.

I stand on my hind legs.

Lolani twirls her fingers in a circle. I start to twirl around.

Around and around and around . . .
Hey, this is fun!

Twirl, twirl, whoa! Maybe not so
fun. I'm getting *wiggle, waggle, dizzy*!

Everything is spinning. The room,
the trees, the two-legs, the . . . Oops!
I just twirled into a dancing two-leg.

Kablam! She's not a dancing two-
leg anymore. She's a sitting two-leg.
(Even though no one gave her the
sign to sit!)

Grumble . . . growl . . . Now she's
a sitting, shouting two-leg. I don't
know what she's saying. But I know
she's saying it to me. And she sounds
really mad.

I cock my head and try to look
cute. But the two-leg doesn't like my
cute face. She's still angry.

Lolani stops waving her hands. She starts yelling at the two-leg who is yelling at me. Then a big two-leg walks over. She points right at me and growls something at Lolani. The big two-leg is loud. And angry.

Lolani points to me and shakes her head.

I don't know what all these two-legs are saying, but I know that it means trouble for me. And trouble is what gets puppies sent to the pound.

I'm not waiting around for *that* to happen. Good-bye, Darla. Good-bye, Willie. Good-bye, Lolani. I am out of here!

CHAPTER 8

Huff, puff, huff. Puff, huff, puff. I've never run up such a big hill before. *Thumpety, thump, thump.* My heart is pounding.

There's a long, skinny water bowl running down the side of this mountain. *Slurp, slurp, slurp.* This water is cold and clean. Not salty like the water in that big ocean.

I look down the mountain. No two-legs have followed me here. I don't see anything but trees and plants below.

Wiggle, waggle, whoopee! My tail

starts doing a happy dance. I'm not going to the pound. There aren't any two-legs up here to put me in one. I'm all alone on the mountain.

Suddenly, my tail stops dancing. It's not so happy anymore. Neither am I. Alone is scary. I don't know where I am. I don't know how to get to the ocean and sand. Which means I don't know how to get to my bone. What if I'm stuck here, *alone*, forever?

"Cheer wee. Cheer wee." Suddenly I hear that birdsong.

Yay! I'm not alone, after all. "Hello, bird buddy!" I bark.

"Cheer wee. Cheer wee."

That's weird. My bird buddy's *cheer wee* doesn't sound cheery. It sounds sad.

"Cheer wee. Cheer wee."

"Don't be sad, bird buddy," I bark back to him. "You're not alone."

"Cheer wee. Cheer wee."

I walk through the bushes, following the sound of my bird buddy's sad song.

"Cheer wee. Cheer wee."

"I'm coming, bird buddy," I bark. "I can hear you. I'm almost . . ."

Oh no!

Now I know why my bird buddy is sad. He's not flying free in the trees. He can't. *He's stuck in a cage.*

I know all about cages with metal bars. I know all about wanting to get out and be free. I know because that was what it was like when I was in the dog pound in London.

My bird buddy is stuck inside a bird *pound*!

And he's not the only one. There are three little yellow-and-green birds in the bird pound. They all look scared.

"Cheer wee. Cheer wee."

Suddenly I hear another bird singing. But his song isn't coming from the cage. It's coming from up high.

My eyes look up. The bird is sitting on a branch in a tree. He's far away from the bird pound.
He's free.

The bird is lucky to have a tree to sit in. There aren't a lot of trees around here. Just a bunch of stumps. Someone has cut down most of the trees. Why would anyone want to do that? Without trees, my bird buddies have no place to build their nests. No place to live.

Except the pound, I guess.

Hey! That bird isn't alone in

the tree. There's a two-leg up there, too. He's holding a stick with a big bag attached to it. Kind of like the bags Josh uses to pick up my poop, except this bag has tiny holes in it. It wouldn't make a good poop bag. But it's the perfect bag for catching a bird. Oh no! I know what's happening now. That isn't any regular two-leg. He's a bird-catching two-leg!

The birdcatcher moves his stick closer to the bird.

"Cheer wee. Cheer wee." The bird flies up

higher in the tree.

"Fly, little bird buddy!" I bark. "Don't let him put you in the bird pound!"

But the bird in the tree doesn't understand me. Birds don't speak dog. And dogs don't speak bird.

The two-leg in the tree doesn't speak dog, either. But he's *definitely* trying to tell me something. He's shouting and waving his arms.

"Cheer wee. Cheer wee."

The birds in the cage sound scared and sad, the same way I felt when I was in the pound.

Thumpety, thump, thump. My heart is pounding hard. What if the birdcatcher is also a dogcatcher? What if he tries to throw me in there, too? I'm too big for that little bird pound. I would get smushed.

I should run away. As fast as I can.

"Cheer wee. Cheer wee."

But I can't leave my bird buddy and his friends in the pound. I have to do something!

The two-leg in the tree starts climbing down. He's coming to get me!

I have to work fast. *Scratch, scratch, scratch.* I use my paw to dig at the door to the cage. But the door doesn't open.

The two-leg is still yelling and waving his big stick at me.

"Come on, door. Come on, door," I bark. *Scratch, scratch, scratch.*

The two-leg is on the ground. He's running toward me.

Thumpety, thump, thump. My
heart is pounding.

Scratch, scratch, scratch. My paw
is moving up and down on the cage
door.

At last, the cage door swings open.

"Cheer wee! Cheer wee." The
birds fly out of the cage and up into
the sky.

The two-leg glares at me. Then
he stares at the birds in the sky. He

starts swinging his stick in the air, trying to catch the birds.

But they are flying way too high. He can't catch them now.

"Cheer wee! Cheer wee!" the birds sing out.

I love hearing their song. But I can't stay. I have to run

as far as I can from the two-leg with the stick.

Because birds aren't the only ones who want to be free! *Zoom, zoom, zoomee!*

CHAPTER 9

The sand! I've found the sand!

I can't believe it. One minute I'm running through the mud and trees and the next I'm back on the sand. Maui sure is *wowie*! But I'm really ready to go home. It's time to dig up my magic bone!

Wiggle, waggle, weird. The little house near where I buried my bone seems a lot closer to the ocean than it did this morning. It's like the ocean is growing. Or the sand is shrinking.

Wiggle, waggle, weirder. There's a

group of two-legs in the ocean. And they're standing on *top* of the water.

Wiggle, waggle, weirdest. One of them is Lolani!

But wait. There's a dog standing on the water, too! And not just any dog. It's Olina. The Shiba Inu I met earlier! The wind is blowing through her fur as she moves up and down on the water. I can tell she's having fun. She's got a big smile on her face. So does the two-leg standing behind her.

Nobody can stand on top of water. I'm sure of

it. But Lolani is doing it. And so is Olina. Right now. Right there.

Uh-oh! A giant wall of water rushes up behind Lolani. It wants to push her down.

"Look out, Lolani! Look out!" I shout to her. But Lolani can't hear me.

The wall of water is rushing faster and faster toward Lolani. I bury my head in my paws. I can't look.

Whoosh! I hear the water rushing up onto the sand. Then it moves away again. It feels like the water is pulling the sand right out from under my paws.

Slowly, I lift my head. I look out at the water. There's Lolani! She's still standing! The water didn't knock her down!

"Yay, Lolani!" I bark excitedly.

Lolani comes out of the water carrying the biggest chew toy I've ever seen. It's taller than she is.

Boy, do I want a bite of that! I know I should just dig up my bone and go home. And I will. Right after I take a couple of nibbles on Lolani's giant chew toy.

I run over and nip at her heels. "Can I have a bite of your chew toy? Can I? Can I?"

Lolani smiles. She lays the chew toy down right at the edge of the water.

Oh boy! Oh boy! She's going to let me take a bite. It's time to chew! *Wiggle, waggle, woo-hoo!*

I jump onto the giant chew toy and get my teeth ready for a good chomp. Lolani lies down on top of the chew toy, too. Suddenly, the chew toy starts moving out into the water— with Lolani and me on top of it!

"No! No!" I bark. "Take me back! Take me back!" But Lolani doesn't paddle us back to the sand. She paddles us farther and farther into the giant ocean.

The water is jumping up and down all around me. It's like being trapped in a cold, salty bath. I hate baths. Especially cold ones.

Wham! A wall of water hits me in my face. It washes up my nose and burns its way down my throat. *Cough, cough, cough.*

Olina looked like she was having fun standing on the water. I don't know why. This isn't any fun at all.

We're moving farther and farther away from the sand. Away from the little wooden house. *Away from my magic bone.*

Lolani is paddling fast. She's going farther into the ocean than any of the other two-legs standing on the water. And we're so far from the sand that the two-legs there look teeny-tiny.

Lolani stands up. She bends her knees and holds her arms straight out. Then she moves her hands up and down and all around, as she stands on top of the water. But this time I'm not sitting up or rolling over. No way. I'll roll right into the water!

Whoosh! Another wall of water comes down on Lolani and me. It snuck up behind us. I never saw it coming.

Owie! The water is burning my eyes and clogging my ears.

"Get me out of this bath!" I bark to Lolani.

But Lolani doesn't answer. She can't. She's not there. The giant wall

of water knocked her down. I don't
see her anywhere. Which means I'm
all alone, in the middle of the ocean.

"Lolani!" I bark.

Just then, I see a two-leg's hand popping up out of the water. And then another.

"Lolani!" I bark again.

Lolani's head pops up for a second. She lets out a sound. But a new wall of water knocks her down again. The giant ocean is swallowing her up. I can see the teeny-tiny two-legs on the sand pointing to us. One of them is running into the water.

The other two-legs in the ocean are paddling toward us now. But they're still far away.

The only one close enough to help Lolani is me! If I can just get this giant chew toy over to her, maybe she can climb up and paddle back.

I start to move my arms and legs back and forth—just like Lolani did. I'm dog-paddling to her.

And then, suddenly, I spot something else. A bone! And not just any bone. It's my magic bone.

I remember the water jumping up

on the sand and then running away again. I remember it pulling the sand back with it. The ocean must have climbed up onto the ground, swallowed the sand near the little house—and *taken my bone with it*!

I'm not going to let the ocean steal my bone away from me. No way. Quickly I start dog-paddling toward my magic bone.

Lolani's head pops up above the water. Her arms swing up, down, and all around. She's shouting something at me, but I don't understand.

Then she goes under again.

I want to help Lolani. But if I dog-paddle toward her, I won't be able to fetch my bone. And I won't ever get home.

But if I dog-paddle to my magic bone, the ocean might swallow Lolani. Then *she* won't ever get home.

Oh no! Which one should I save?

CHAPTER 10

Lolani is my friend. She gave me pineapple pieces. She shared her shave ice. And she didn't yell at me when I caused trouble in school. I can't let the ocean swallow her! I have to save her. Even if it means I can never go home again.

I can't think about that now. I just have to keep moving.

Paddle, paddle, paddle. My paws try to run in the water. But it's hard to go fast.

Lolani's head pops up. Then it

goes under the water again.

Paddle, paddle, paddle. Hold on, Lolani. I'm coming.

Lolani's arms fly up over the water. I paddle as hard as I can. I want to reach Lolani before another big wall of water comes.

"I'm here! I'm here!" I bark to Lolani. "I'm right next to you."

Lolani doesn't know what I'm saying, but she sees her giant chew toy. She puts her arms over the board and pulls herself up.

Just in time. Another big wall of water is coming right for us.

"Hold on tight, Lolani," I bark. "Hold on . . ."

I stop midbark. Because from the corner of my eye I spy something wonderful. Something amazing.

MY MAGIC BONE! It's here, floating near us.

But before I can reach it, the ocean begins to carry it away from me again.

No way. I'm not letting that happen. My bone isn't getting away from me this time. Quickly, I leap into the water and swim to my bone.

I grab my magic bone between my teeth. I look over at Lolani. She has climbed onto her chew toy and is safe. She can paddle back to the sand. She can go home.

I taste my meaty magic bone. I can go home, too. Right now. All I have to do is . . . *Chomp*!

Wiggle, waggle, whew. I feel dizzy—like my insides are spinning all around—but my outsides are standing still. Stars are twinkling in front of my eyes—even though it's daytime! All around me I smell food—fried chicken, salmon, roast beef. But there isn't any food in sight.

Kaboom! Kaboom! Kaboom!

A minute later, the *kaboom*ing stops. Just like that. I look around.

There's my tree! My fence! The flowers I dug up this morning! And best of all, my house!

I wonder what Josh would do if he saw my magic bone. Would he take a bite? Where would he go? What if he didn't know how to get back to me? I don't want Josh to leave me. I better hide my bone so he can't find it.

Diggety, dig, dig. I dig another big hole, right near the flower bed. I bury my bone in there.

I look down. The grass is still tied around my middle. I have to get that off! What if the neighborhood dogs—or worse yet, Queenie, the neighborhood cat—sees me wearing grass? They all would laugh at me.

I wriggle around in the mud. The grass doesn't budge.

I bite at the string. The grass is still there.

I scratch my back against my tree. Finally, *snap*! The string breaks in two and the grass falls to the ground. I bury it with my bone. No one will ever know I once wore grass.

Then I remember that I still have the circle of red and yellow flowers around my neck. But I'm not going to bury them in a hole. I'm putting the flowers on top of Josh's flower bed to replace the ones I *duggety, dug, dug* up this morning.

I hear something outside the yard. It's Josh's machine—the one with four paws. Josh is home!

My paws race to him. Fast. Faster. *Fastest!*

My fur falls down in my eyes. I can't see where I'm running. But my paws keep going. Fast. Faster. *Boom*!

My paws run right into Josh! But he doesn't get mad. He just smiles

and scratches my ears.

Just then, Josh spots something near the back of the yard. He stops scratching, gets up, and walks over to his flower bed. He picks up the big circle of flowers and gives me a funny look.

I wish I could tell Josh where I got the flowers. I wish I could tell him about Lolani, and the *cheer-wee* birds, and the yummy shave ice. Most of all, I wish I could tell him how happy I am to be home with him again.

But I can't. Because Josh doesn't speak dog. And I don't speak two-leg. So I just reach out my tongue and give him a big lick.

I think he understands.

Fun Facts About Sparky's Adventures in Hawaii

Lei

This traditional Hawaiian necklace made of flowers is given as a gift to say *welcome, congratulations,* or *I love you.*

Hula

Hawaiians have been dancing the hula for hundreds of years. This type of dance is actually a form of storytelling. Hula dancers use their body motions to tell a story about things that happened in Hawaii a long time ago.

Hawaii

The state of Hawaii is made up of eight different islands, all of which were formed by volcanoes. The Hawaiian Islands are Hawai'i, Kaho'olawe, Kaua'i, Lana'i, Maui, Moloka'i, Ni'iahu, and O'ahu.

Maui Parrotbill

This bird isn't a parrot at all. It's actually a member of the finch family. There were once many Maui parrotbills in Hawaii, but now there are only about five hundred left. It is now illegal to capture and sell Maui parrotbills because they are an endangered species.

Poi

Poi is a traditional Hawaiian food made from the root of the taro plant. It is thick and pastelike, kind of like porridge. Only you don't eat poi with a spoon. You eat it with your fingers! Poi can be sweet, but it tastes and smells more sour with age.

Shave Ice

Hawaiian shave ice is a dessert made by shaving pieces from a large block of ice and covering the ice shavings with syrup made from fruits grown in Hawaii, such as pineapple, guava, or coconut.

Surfing

Hawaiians have been using surfboards to ride the waves of the Pacific Ocean for a long time. Ancient Hawaiians carved pictures of surfers into lava rocks, and there are chants and songs about surfers that can be traced back more than five hundred years.

About the Author

Nancy Krulik is the author of more than 200 books for children and young adults, including three *New York Times* Best Sellers. She is best known for being the author and creator of several successful book series for children, including Katie Kazoo, Switcheroo; How I Survived Middle School; and George Brown, Class Clown. Nancy lives in Manhattan with her husband, composer Daniel Burwasser, and her crazy beagle mix, Josie, who manages to drag her along on many exciting adventures without ever leaving Central Park.

About the Illustrator

You could fill a whole attic with Seb's drawings! His collection includes some very early pieces made when he was four—there is even a series of drawings he did at the movies in the dark! When he isn't doodling, he likes to make toys and sculptures, as well as bows and arrows for his two boys, Oscar and Leo, and their numerous friends. Seb is French and lives in England. His website is www.sebastienbraun.com.